Red Light, Green Lion

Each day holds a surprise. But only if we expect it can we see, hear, or feel it when it comes to us. Let's not be afraid to receive each day's surprise, whether it comes to us as sorrow or as joy. It will open a new place in our hearts, a place where we can welcome friends and celebrate more fully our shared humanity.

— Henri Nouwen

For Henri Nouwen, who taught me how to look for the hidden gifts in rainy-day red lights. — C.R.

For Jean-Philippe, my dear blue lion. It certainly was worth the wait!
And with many thanks to Rick and Debbie, for ... well, for everything. — J.Y.

Text © 2019 Candace Ryan
Illustrations © 2019 Jennifer Yerkes

Kids Can Press gratefully acknowledges the financial support of the Government of Ontario, through the Ontario Media Development Corporation, for our publishing activity.

Published in Canada and the U.S. by Kids Can Press Ltd.
25 Dockside Drive, Toronto, ON M5A 0B5

Kids Can Press is a Corus Entertainment Inc. company

www.kidscanpress.com

The artwork in this book was rendered in Caran d'Ache Neocolor II pastels and Tombow Dual Brush pen.
The text is set in Minik.

Edited by Debbie Rogosin
Designed by Marie Bartholomew

Printed and bound in Shenzhen, China, in 10/2018 by C & C Offset

CM 19 0 9 8 7 6 5 4 3 2 1

Library and Archives Canada Cataloguing in Publication

Ryan, Candace, author
    Red light, green lion / Candace Ryan ; illustrated by Jennifer Yerkes.
ISBN 978-1-5253-0015-8 (hardcover)
I. Yerkes, Jennifer, illustrator II. Title.
PZ7.R9477Red 2019   j813'.6   C2018-902009-1

Red Light, Green Lion

Written by Candace Ryan

Illustrated by Jennifer Yerkes

Kids Can Press

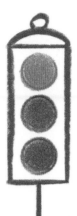

Some days are not like most days.

Red light, green li-

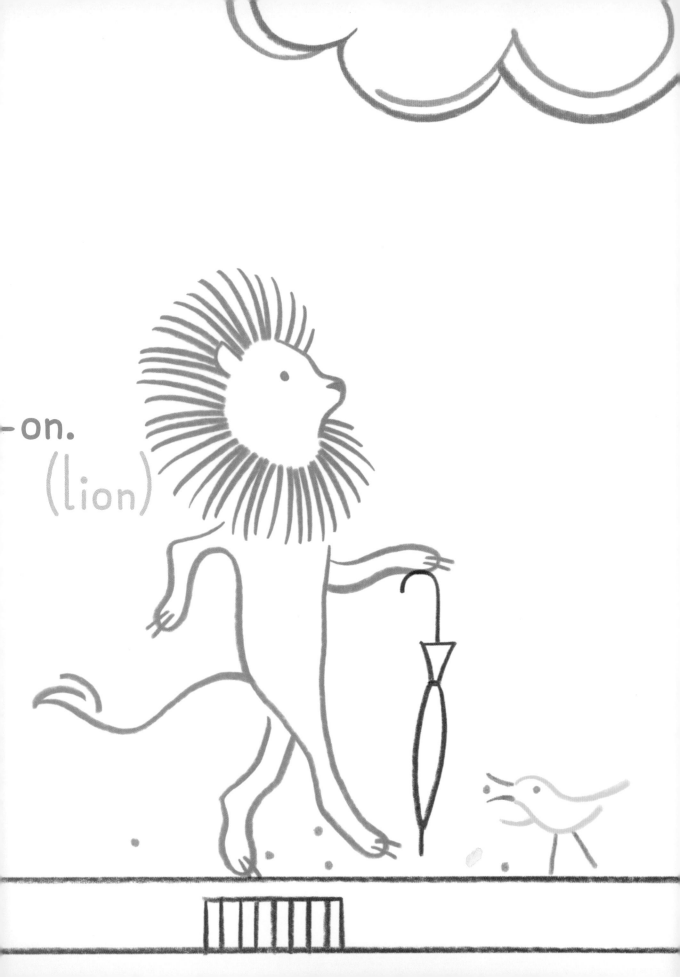

-on.
(lion)

Some days are full of surprises.

Red light, green li-

-ghtning!
(lightning)

Yikes!

So it's always good to be prepared.

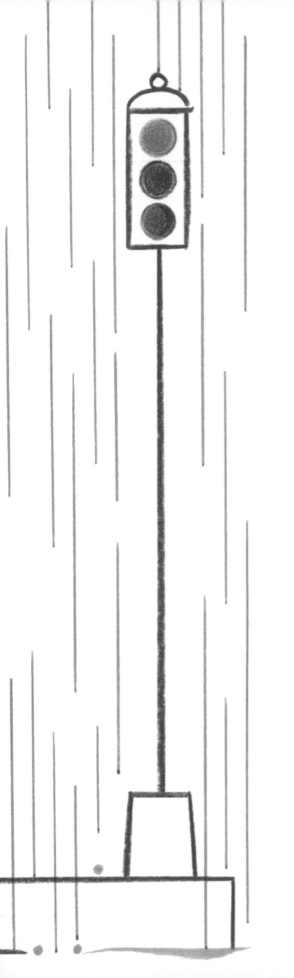

Some days, we find
tiny things that
need tender care.

Red light, green li-

-lac.

(lilac)

Some days, we
get exactly what
we need, exactly
when we need it.

Red light, green li-

Whew!

-fesaver.
(lifesaver)

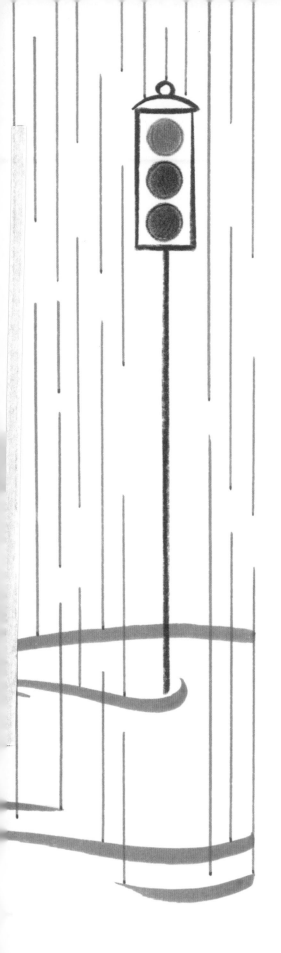

And some days, nothing goes the way we thought it would. But then something happens that makes the journey easier.

Red light, green li-

-feboat.
(lifeboat)

Some days, we meet others in need.

Red light, green li-

-vestock.
(livestock)

And we can choose
to show kindness.

Some days,
everything slows down, and we
may feel stuck. Those are good
times to be still and think.

Red light, green li-

-brary books.

(library books)

Some days bring things that
are silly and strange and
seem to make no sense at all.

Red light, green li-

-ma beans.
(lima beans)

Then, on some days, when we feel most discouraged, something amazing happens right in front of us, and we don't even notice it happening.

Red light, green li-

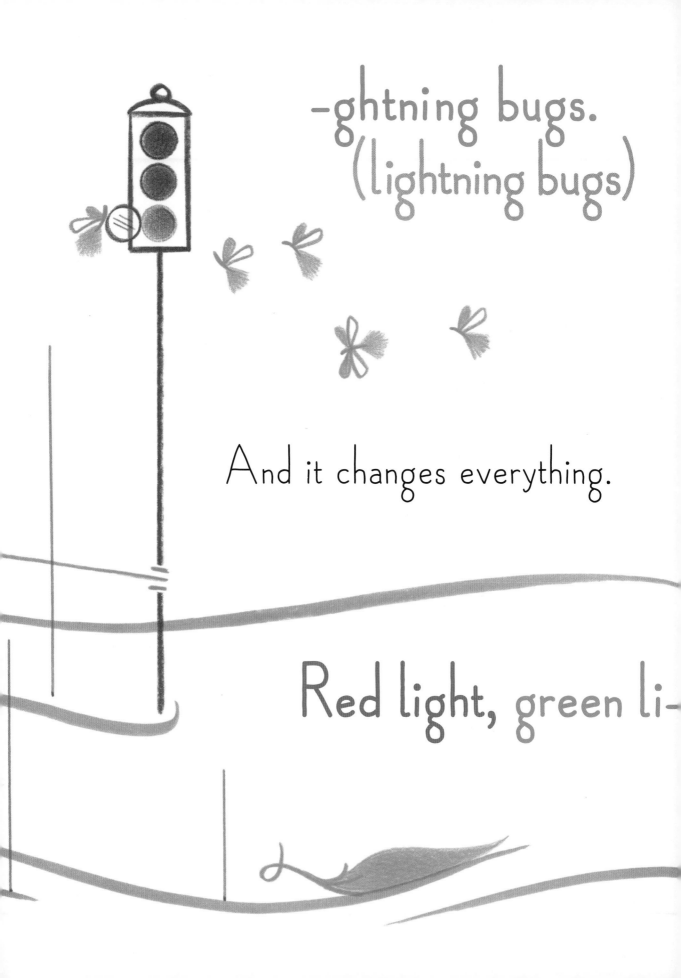

-ghtning bugs.
(lightning bugs)

And it changes everything.

Red light, green li-

-ght.
(light)

Green light?!?
Green light!!!

Line dance!

Some days don't make much sense in the beginning.

Red li-

-on,
(lion)

green li-

-on.
(lion)

But they always make

sense in the end.